Cat Ears on ELIZABETH

written by
Rachel Vail

illustrated by
Paige Keiser

Feiwel and Friends
New York

A FEIWEL AND FRIENDS BOOK
An imprint of Macmillan Publishing Group, LLC
120 Broadway, New York, NY 10271

Our books may be purchased in bulk for promotional,
educational, or business use. Please contact your local
bookseller or the Macmillan Corporate and Premium Sales
Department at (800) 221-7945 ext. 5442 or by email
at MacmillanSpecialMarkets@macmillan.com.

Library of Congress Control Number: 2019948759
ISBN 978-1-250-16220-5

Book design by Liz Dresner
Feiwel and Friends logo designed by Filomena Tuosto

First edition, 2020
1 3 5 7 9 10 8 6 4 2
mackids.com

To Carin, brilliant friend and artist—with walks, rants, love, and celebrations. Let's keep solving everything together. —R.V.

For Bradley —P.K.

Chapter
1

In second grade, we all look great!

It is not only Mallory who looks great.

That's what Ms. Patel says.

Ms. Patel is our Class 2B teacher.

She is very beautiful.

She has mooshy-gooshy arms.

She has smile-crinkles near her eyes.

And earrings. Sometimes she has a barrette in her hair.

We all look different, Ms. Patel said yesterday.

But everybody in the whole second grade looks GREAT!

Mallory has glitter folders and bright orange sneakers and a huge pink eraser.

And Mallory has cat ears on her headband.

Chapter 2

Today Anna came to school with cat ears on her headband, too.

She was showing it off to everybody, all day.

"You look great," Mallory told Anna.

"We both do!" said Anna. "We both look great!"

They jumped around in a circle holding hands, yelling, "Don't we look great?"

"Yes!" Bucky told them. "You look like cats! I love cats!"

Bucky is my best friend.

He did not say I look like a cat.

He did not say I look great.

Cat ears on your headband is not the only way to look great.

But it is a very good way.

Chapter 3

I don't have cat ears on my anything.

I don't have any headband at all.

Mine got lost.

Headbands squish my brains out.

That's why I had to take it off so much.

And then I don't know what happened to it.

It wasn't my fault.

My unsquished head felt very naked and not-great the whole large recess time today.

Chapter 4

"I need a cat-ears headband!" I told Mom after school.

"A what?" she asked.

"Right away!" I yelled. "I NEED one!"

"Elizabeth," Mom said. She said it like *Eeeeee-lizzzz-ahhhh-bethhhhh*.

She says my name soooo slowly
when she does not understand that
something is an emergency.

"This is an emergency," I explained.
"We have to go to the headband store
right away!"

"Buckle your seat belt," said Mom.

I did.

I buckled right up for speeding to the headband store.

"Do we have a siren and red swirly lights on our car?" I asked.

Sirens and red swirly lights make cars go very fast.

Like police and fire trucks and an ambulance.

Chapter
5

We did not have those things.

Mom is a slow driver, with a lot of looking in the mirrors and windows.

Sometimes I forget which is windows and which is mirrors.

A mirror is the same as a window, except it's just you again, on both sides.

The window of the car looked like I was outside, riding along, with a stormy-Elizabeth face.

This is why mirrors and windows are confusing.

"I need! A cat-ears! Headband!" I yelled at outside-me, who also didn't have one.

"You said headbands squish your brains out," Mom said.

"That was when I was younger," I said. "My skull is stronger now."

"That was two weeks ago," said Mom.

"When I was two weeks younger!" I explained.

"She is very hardheaded," said my brother, Justin.

"Thank you, Justin," I said.

Mom made breathing noises.

"I can bang this hard head against the window and show you," I offered.

Mom said, "NO."

Chapter 6

punt!

Mom also said NO to getting a cat-ears headband.

"*NO* is your favorite word," I said.

"Elizabeth," Mom said. "There is no reason to be nasty."

"Ever?" I asked.

"Ever," Mom said.

"What about the rule of Tell the Truth?" I asked.

Mom looked at me with the mirror. "It's not lying if you keep a mean thought to yourself. You're allowed  to think anything, inside the privacy of your own strong head."

So the rest of the way home, I kept that mean thought inside my own strong head:

NO *is Mom's favorite word.*

I thought it over and over without stopping:

NO *is Mom's favorite word* NO *is Mom's favorite word* NO

It was such a loud, angry sentence I couldn't even hear the music Mom turned on.

Chapter
7

We went straight home instead of to the headband store.

I went straight up to my room to sulk.

I was keeping and keeping my mean thought inside my strong head for possible use later.

In case Mom was wrong and there sometimes is a reason to be nasty, I wanted to have it ready.

I wrote it down:

MOM NO

on an index card and hid it under my
socks.

Writing it down was still keeping it
to myself, even though it was outside
my strong head.

Chapter
8

My stuffed dog-rabbit, Dolores, and my Really Dog, Qwerty, tried to cuddle me up.

They thought I looked great.

But they never saw how great I would look in a cat-ears headband.

I made a wish:

Please, somebody give me a cat-ears headband to wear to school tomorrow so I will look great like Mallory and Anna.

Dolores and Qwerty had no cat-ears headbands, or they would share.

They didn't have any ideas to share, either.

Chapter 9

I had a great idea!

All by myself!

Well, with the help of my eyes.

My eyes saw an important thing on
my desk.

It was: GLUE!

I have glue! And other art things!

We could *make* me a cat-ears headband!

I have trouble with glue because it always comes out not enough and then too much.

But Mom and Dad are very good at gluing.

All I had to do was find cat ears!

And a headband!

Because I already have glue!

Chapter
10

I found so many things in my closet,
when I emptied it into my room.

I found my old stuffty named
Marina and also that nightgown I love
that I forgot about!

I found my favorite old doll named
Harry! Or maybe it was Joan.

I found my play phone that is also a calculator.

I sat down on my pile of everything and called my imaginary friends.

Their names are Mrs. Noodleman and Mr. Noodleman.

I told Mrs. Noodleman and Mr. Noodleman about the cat-ears-headband emergency.

You are right, Elizabeth, said Mrs. Noodleman. *You would look great in a cat-ears headband!*

You would not lose it like all those old headbands, said Mr. Noodleman.

Those headbands did not have cat ears on them, Mrs. Noodleman said.

Good point, Mrs. Noodleman, said Mr. Noodleman.

Thank you. Good-bye, I said to the Noodlemans.

Chapter 11

"I have a great idea," I told the Really
People in my family at dinner.

"Uh-oh," said Dad.

"No glitter," said Mom.

"You're in luck!" I told them. "This
great idea has no glitter! Only glue
and a headband! And cat ears!"

"Glue?" asked Dad.

"Glue is the part I already have!" I told his worried face.

"Did you find any of your headbands?" asked Mom.

"Not yet," I said. "So that is one problem with my idea. The other problem is, do any of you have spare cat ears?"

"I'd have to check my toolbox," Dad said. "Ouch! What?"

Mom was giving Dad an angry look.

"Just kidding, Elizabeth," Dad said. "No, I have no cat ears. Sorry."

I slumped in my chair. "You didn't even check your toolbox."

"You can have pigtails tomorrow," Mom said. "That'll be easier than trying to make our own cat-ears headband. Less of a mess."

Chapter 12

Fiona has pigtails.

Fiona is in 2B. She is very quiet, but she is smart, and her pigtails look cute.

Cali sometimes has pigtails, too.

We don't call

her Babyish Cali anymore because that is not nice.

Pigtails might look great on me. But I want to be a cat, not a pig.

"Or maybe braids," I said.

"Okay," Mom said. "Now eat your dinner."

I pushed my peas away from my rice. I do not like when foods touch each other.

I was thinking about braids. Zora sometimes has braids. I like her braids.

Getting braids yanks my head-skin.

Braids make my face feel very stretched to the sides.

"Or a baseball cap," I suggested.

Sometimes Bucky wears a baseball cap.

"Sure," Mom said.
"Whatever you want.
Have some dinner now."
Sometimes Ms. Patel
wears a barrette in
her hair.
"Or a barrette," I said.
"Okay!" Mom said.
We both smiled, because of being
proud of me.

Chapter 13

Some of us were less proud of me after they saw the State of my room.

"Your room is a State," Dad said.

I did not know that fact before.

I had to clean it up, with only a little help.

Then I had to have a bath and my hair washed.

I didn't want to do that, either.

"You don't have to like it. You just have to do it," said Mom.

That might be a mean thing Mom just said, I thought.

Mean Mom, I thought at her.

But I kept those thoughts inside my strong private head.

Chapter 14

When I looked at Clean Elizabeth in
the mirror, I knew the truth.

A cap is nothing.

With a cap on, I would not look like
a cat at all.

I wouldn't even look like Bucky.

With pigtails, I wouldn't look like a piggy, or like Cali or Fiona.

With a barrette in my hair, I wouldn't look like Ms. Patel.

Or a cat, which is what would look great.

I would just look like Elizabeth, with a barrette.

Which is nothing.

I always look like just Elizabeth.

What I needed was to look like somebody else.

Somebody who looks great.

Like Mallory.

Chapter 15

Exactly what I needed was:

1. A cat-ears headband

Exactly what I did not have:

1. A cat-ears anything
2. An anything headband
3. A good feeling about my day ahead

Chapter
16

"No thanks," I said, when Mom tried to barrette my hair.

"Why not?" she asked. "I thought you wanted special hair today."

"It's not the same," I explained.

"No," Mom said. "But different is fine! Different is terrific!"

"Not in Class 2B," I said.

"Everywhere!" said Dad.

"You don't get it," I said.

"That's my waffle," said Justin.

Chapter 17

I was using the waffle as a berry-smoosher.

My waffle.

It used to be Justin's but not anymore.

He is too slow an eater. It drives me bonkers.

"Stop playing with your food," Dad said.

"It's Justin's food," I said.

"You can keep it now," said Justin.

"Even berries want to be the same," I explained.

"The same as what?" Mom asked.

"They say they're BLUEberries or BLACKberries," I said. "But see? They are all *purpleberries* when squish comes to shove."

"Ew," said Justin.

"IT IS AN EXPRESSION!" I explained calmly, with my teeth all purple like a monster.

Chapter 18

Waiting for the bus, I pretended my imaginaries were with me instead of my brother.

You're a purpleberry, I imagined Mrs. Noodleman saying to Mr. Noodleman.

You're a purpleberry, I imagined
Mr. Noodleman saying back.

They tease each other but not in a
mean way.

And their feelings don't get
squished into purple.

Chapter
19

I sat on the bus to school next to my best friend, Bucky.

"Don't tease me today," I said to Bucky.

"Okay," said Bucky.

"My feelings are tender today," I explained.

"Sometimes that happens," said
Bucky.

Bucky is a good choice as a best
friend.

I don't know who Mallory's best
friend is.

Chapter 20

Cali had a cat-ears headband on, too.

At lunch, Mallory and Anna and
Cali were all meowing.

"I'm allergic to cats," I told them.

My sandwich was dented.

Just like my feelings.

Chapter 21

Class 2B went outside in the afternoon!

Usually we are in Class 2B but we lined up and out we went.

"Wherever we go, we are still Class 2B," Ms. Patel told us on our way.

We went all the way to the huge tree at the back of the field.

We were collecting leaves!

Each kid in Class 2B gets to choose three beautiful leaves!

"This tree is such a nice place to visit," said Ms. Patel, looking up at it.

I looked up at it, too.

"It is nice," I said. "But I would actually rather visit the cat-ears-headband store."

Ms. Patel smiled at me and said, "Just looking at this tree's leaves, and its reaching branches, and its craggy bark, well, that soothes loud feelings."

"I have very loud feelings!" I said.

"I know you do, Elizabeth," Ms. Patel said.

"How about you, Ms. Patel?" I asked. "Do you have loud feelings, too?"

"Yes," Ms. Patel said. "Sometimes I do."

I never knew that before about teachers having loud feelings.

"Wow," I said.

aspen

sea buckthorn

apple

oak

Chapter 22

We are going to make a class project.

Everybody will work on it together.

That will make it beautiful.

The project is something called a collage.

We know what a collage is already, because we are in second grade, not kindergarten.

A collage is not a fancy way of saying the name for sleepaway school when you are big.

That is something else.

I was mostly joking when I said, "A collage is sleepaway school for when you're big."

A collage is:

You glue things on the big paper and it is a mess.

I remember that now!

I love doing a collage!

I got one small leaf and two bigs.

We all showed our leaves to each other.

Anybody whose leaf wasn't

beautiful enough dropped that one
and chose a new one.

"Beautiful!" Ms. Patel kept saying
when we showed her our leaves.
"Beautiful!"

Chapter 23

My grandparents Gingy and Poopsie
are babysitting us.

"Look at you in your swanky
clothes," Gingy said to Mom and Dad,
and took a picture.

Justin got in the picture with them
but I didn't want to.

Usually Gingy and Poopsie
babysitting makes me feel twirly.

They like games like Trick or Treat,
and Library, and Disgusting Dessert
Shop.

Those are my three favorite games,
too.

But tonight I was down in the
dumps.

Because I remembered a terrible thing:

There are no cat ears on me.

I didn't want to be in any pictures.

I didn't even want to taste the Disgusting Dessert.

I had a little, so I wouldn't hurt their feelings.

But not as much as I wanted.

Not as much as I would have if I were UP in the dumps.

Chapter
24

"Do you want something else?"
Poopsie asked me.

"Yes," I said, because it is a rule in
my family: *Tell the Truth*.

"Some Jell-O?" Gingy asked.

"Gingy can make you Jell-O,"
Poopsie said. "Elizabeth wants Jell-O!"

"No, I do not want any Jell-O," I said.

"Who wouldn't want Jell-O?" Poopsie asked. "It is very jiggly!"

"Not everybody likes food that jiggles," said Justin.

"Everybody likes jiggly food!" Poopsie insisted.

"Different people like different things," Gingy said. "What do *you* want, Elizabeth?"

"I want a headband with cat ears on it."

"And Jell-O!" Poopsie said.

"No thanks," I said. "I just want the headband and that's all. But I can't have it."

"Why not?" Gingy asked.

"Because she loses all her headbands," Justin explained.

"Only in the PAST!" I yelled. "You can't predict the FUTURE!"

"The future is the hardest thing to predict," Gingy said.

Chapter
25

Uh-oh!

Fiona's birthday party!

We had to get ready fast.

We had to stop at the
toy store on the way.

"We should just buy
a bunch of presents and

keep them in the closet," Mom said to Dad. "We always have to rush on the way to the party!"

"We could keep all the presents in the State of My Room," I said.

"In the what?" Mom asked.

"Daddy said my room is a State," I said. "Like Alaska, and Mississippi. And My Room."

"That's an expression, silly goose," Mom said. "Hurry and pick something."

Mom's favorite word is NO but her second favorite is HURRY.

I kept that mean sentence inside my private head, too.

Chapter
26

There are so many wonderful things in the toy store.

I wish I could live in the toy store, choosing and choosing.

I held a cat-ears headband in my hand.

"Maybe we should get this for me,"

 I suggested to Mom. "To wear to Fiona's party."

"We're just buying a present for Fiona right now," Mom said. "Do you want to buy that for Fiona?"

Fiona doesn't talk very much.

Maybe she would like to meow.

She would probably like a cat-ears headband.

I chose a puzzle instead.

Maybe Fiona likes puzzles.

It's not fair if she has a cat-ears headband and I do not.

Chapter
27

Fiona's party was: paint a flowerpot and while that dries, eat pizza.

Then fill the pot with dirt and choose a lump called a "bulb."

Shove the bulb into the dirt in the pot.

Maybe that is Fiona's hobby. I don't know.

Birthday parties and other people's houses are sometimes strange.

"Try not to make such a mess," said Fiona's dad.

"Dirt is dirty," Mallory whispered.

"Yeah," I said. "That's the truest thing about dirt!"

Mallory smudged some dirt on her nose.

I smudged some on mine.

Chapter
28

Mallory and I had to go wash up
before cake.

Fiona's dad said, "Shoes!" as we
walked into the house.

"Why did he just yell *shoes*?"
Mallory whispered to me.

"Maybe it's an expression," I said.

"An expression?" she asked.

"That's when you say nonsense," I explained. "My family has a lot of those."

"Mine too," Mallory said.

"It's a little confusing, honestly," I said.

"I agree!" Mallory said. "You're so smart, Elizabeth!"

"Thank you," I said politely. "I know a lot of expressions."

"A lot of nonsense?" Mallory asked.

"Yes," I said. "I'll teach you so much nonsense, if you want."

"Great!" Mallory said. "Learning new things is great!"

We looked in the mirror at our faces. They both had nose smudges.

"We look like puppies!" Mallory said.

"Woof woof!" I said.

"Woof woof!" Mallory answered.

We laughed and washed our hands but kept our nose smudges because we were being puppies together.

Woof Woof!

Chapter
29

"Woof woof!" Mallory said to Anna.

"Meow," Anna said.

"Meow," said Mallory.

"Happy birthday, Fiona!" sang all of Fiona's grown-ups.

"Meow meow meow meow

meowwwww," sang Anna and Mallory and Cali.

I didn't sing along because I was the kind of animal that has no meows at all.

Chapter
30

Today is not my birthday.

Today is just a regular Sunday.

But when Gingy and Poopsie came over, they had a present for me!

It was a box with a bow on top of it!

And *wrapping paper*!

It was an I LOVE YOU present.

I never knew there was a kind of
present called an I LOVE YOU present
before today.

That is okay.

Learning new things is great!

So is a present with the name
ELIZABETH on it!

Chapter
31

I was careful with the wrapping paper but then I wasn't.

While I unwrapped, I sang a song called "My Opening My I Love You Present Song."

That song goes:

I love you!
I love you!
I love Gingy and Poopsie!
And Gingy and Poopsie love me!
And I! LOVE! I LOVE YOU!
PRESENTS!!!

All that happiness came before I
even got the box open and saw what
was inside.

A CAT-EARS HEADBAND!

For ME!!!!!!

Chapter
33

"Just what you wanted!" Gingy said. "Right?"

"Um, yes!" I said, looking closer at that I Love You present.

My new headband looked a little different from Mallory's.

Mallory's and Anna's and Cali's
each have two pointy black ears.

Mine had two soft floofy
ears, black and white, and
two brown pointy ones.

"Hooray!" said
Gingy. "We went
right to the store this
morning on our walk!
Try it on!"

Chapter
34

I tried it on.

"Do I look great?" I asked Gingy
and Poopsie.

"You look FANTASTIC!" said
Poopsie, looking at me proudly.

"You always look great," said
Gingy. She clapped a few times.

I looked in the mirror to see if they were right.

I wasn't sure.

Chapter
35

After a little while I had to take off
my cat-ears headband to rest my
squished head.

Sometimes even hardheaded
second graders have heads that have
to get used to it.

That is not called being babyish.

I didn't lose my new cat-ears
headband.

I just couldn't find it for a little
while.

Chapter
36

But then I did find it, right under my cape and blanket.

Phew.

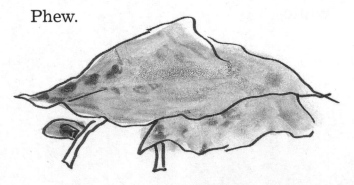

Chapter
37

After bedtime, my stuffed dog-rabbit, Dolores, squinted at my new headband with her one eye.

"Those are cat ears, right?" I asked Dolores.

Dolores didn't answer.

"A kind of cat ears," I said.

Dolores didn't answer.

"There are many types of cats," Mrs. Noodleman whispered.

"Mrs. Noodleman knows everything," said Mr. Noodleman.

But Dolores and I weren't sure anymore.

"This is cat ears, right?" I asked my brother, Justin, while we walked to the bus stop.

He looked sad and doubting at me.

"A kind of cat ears?"

Justin shook his head.

He is in fifth grade, and very smart.

"Are they cow ears?" I asked.

"Yes," he said.

"Really? They have to be COW ears? Definitely?"

"They're cow ears," Justin said.

"Maybe there is a kind of cat that has cow ears," I tried.

"And cow horns?" asked Justin.

"Just because a person is in fifth grade doesn't mean he knows every kind of cat," I said.

"What?" Justin asked. "I didn't say . . ."

"IT'S AN EXPRESSION," I yelled at him.

"Okay," Justin said.

Chapter 39

I walked a few steps away.

I waited for the bus NOT next to that know-it-all brother anymore.

While I waited, I thought about throwing my new headband in the grass and losing it.

I imagined Gingy's face and Poopsie's face.

Their happy faces when they gave me this headband.

Their sad faces if I lost it the first day.

I imagined Mom's face if I said the words, "I lost it."

Or even the true words of "I threw it in the grass because it was cow ears."

But then it was time to get on the bus, and have people tease me for a cow-ears headband.

Chapter 40

"Hey, you look great!" Bucky said.

"Do I, though?" I asked.

"Cow ears!" he said. "I love cows!"

I slumped down low in my seat.

"Look!" Bucky said, and pointed to his arm. "Cow Band-Aid!"

"Cool," I said.

"We're twins!" Bucky said.

"Yeah!" I said.

Twins is good. Twins is, it's not only you being a cow.

Twins means you are exactly like somebody, so you're not alone.

Bucky is my best friend.

But I also wanted to be twins with Anna and mostly Mallory.

Not just Bucky.

Chapter
41

All morning I wore
my cow-ears
headband.

Nobody
teased me.

I tried to
feel great in it.

Chapter 42

The not-teasing ended at recess.

"Hey, Elizabeth," Mallory yelled.
"Are you supposed to be a cow?"

"Meow," said Anna.

"Meow," said Cali.

"Meow," said Rose, who is in Class
2A, so who even knows her?

But she had a cat-ears headband,
too, at recess.

Nobody else had a cow-ears
headband.

Chapter
43

"You have to say MOO," said Mallory, pointing her finger right in my face.

"Moo!" said Bucky. "Moo, moo!"

"*Elizabeth* has to say MOO," said Mallory. "Elizabeth is the one who is a COW!"

I thought about if I wanted to say
MOO.

I did not.

I wanted to say something mean, to
make Mallory feel as bad as she was
making me feel.

Or else something like meow.

Meow is really the only thing I
wished I could be saying.

Chapter
44

But I couldn't.

I had no cat ears.

I took my cow-ears headband off
and walked alone toward the huge tree.

It is a good tree to look at when
you are having loud feelings, Ms. Patel
said.

There is no reason to say mean
things, Mom said.

Chapter 45

I stopped under the tree.

I told myself to keep my angry
sentences inside my private head.

Look at that nice bark, I told
myself. *And those reaching branches.*

*Look at those pretty leaves up there,
turning so many different colors.*

I must feel calm and happy, now!

What I did not feel:

1. Calm
2. Happy

What I did feel:

1. Sad
2. Left out
3. Embarrassed
4. Angry
5. Head-squished from the tight headband morning
6. Like Mallory had followed me

Because there she was, with her cat-ears headband right on her head.

Chapter
46

I turned around to be mean at Mallory.

I yelled, "So what, Mallory? So? I got a cow-ears headband from my Gingy and Poopsie!"

"From your what and what?" Mallory asked.

"My Gingy and Poopsie!" My voice was as loud as my feelings.

They couldn't stay inside me any longer.

She asked, "Those are their really names?"

"Yes," I said. "And they are very excellent people, you standy-uppy-hair Meanie!"

Mallory stopped smiling but she didn't say sorry.

I was still having very loud feelings, so I yelled very loud, "Maybe they gave me a silly headband but it was an I Love You present! And at least I have clean hair!"

"I have clean hair, too," said Mallory.

"It doesn't look clean," I said.

Which was true, but mean. And I knew it.

"It is very clean!" she yelled.

"It is not!" I yelled back. "It's DIRTY!"

"It is so clean there's still shampoo in it!" Mallory yelled even louder.

"Why?" I asked in a quieter voice.

Because, why was there still shampoo in Mallory's hair at recess?

Chapter 47

Mallory took off her cat-ears
headband and itched her hair.

"You don't know why there's
shampoo in your hair?" I asked her.

Mallory shrugged one shoulder.

"Did you have a shampoo accident

in Class 2B this morning when nobody
was looking?" I whispered.

"No," she said. "It was last night,
at home."

She looked very sad.

"What happened?" I asked her.

"My mom wanted to rinse the
shampoo out of my hair and I fussed
and fussed because I didn't want to.
Because I don't like when it gets in
my eyes."

"That's the worst," I agreed.

Mallory nodded. "And my mom said *Fine, then*."

"She let you NOT rinse it out?" I asked.

"Yeah," Mallory said.

"Wow," I said. "My mom never says *Fine, then*. She says, *You don't have to like it, you just have to do it*."

"Yeah," Mallory said. "That never happened to me before, either, her saying *Fine, then*."

I nodded. We both just stood there, thinking about that, about a mom just saying *Fine, then*. "Maybe it was an expression," I said.

"Maybe," said Mallory. "But anyway, now I have Shampoo Head."

"That's so cool," I said.

"It's actually very itchy," she said.

"Oh," I said.

"But, Elizabeth. It is NOT dirty. And it's mean if you say it's dirty."

Chapter 48

Maybe I got soothed from being under the tree.

Maybe my head unsquished.

I don't know.

But my feelings felt much softer.

"So actually your hair is super clean," I said. "And it looks like Lion Hair!"

"It does?" Mallory asked.

"Yeah!"

"I thought it maybe looked terrible," she whispered.

"No," I told her. "You always look great."

"I tried to smoosh it with my cat-ears headband," Mallory said. "But it's getting itchier and itchier."

"You should make it standy-uppier!" I said.

"Like this?" she asked, floofing her hair way up.

"Yes!" I said. "Now roar like a
lion!"

She did.

Chapter
49

"Why are you roaring at Elizabeth?"
Bucky asked Mallory.

"I'm a lion," Mallory said.

"A friendly lion or a
dangerous lion?" Cali
asked her.

"Friendly," I said.

"Meow," said Anna. "Meow, meow."

I straightened my cow-ears headband. "Moo," I said.

"ROAR," said Mallory. Then she held out her cat-ears headband to me. "Want to try it on?"

Chapter
50

I looked at the headband in Mallory's hand.

With the cat ears pointing up so perfectly on the top.

The exact headband I had been wanting so badly.

"No thanks," I said. "Headbands squish my brains out."

"But you have a headband on," said Mallory.

I took mine off and looked at it.

"It's great," Mallory said.

"Is it?" I asked her.

I kept my nasty thoughts about my cow-ears headband inside my private head.

"You're the only one who has a cow headband," Mallory whispered. "So, it's special."

"Oh," I said. "I didn't think of it that way."

"And it was an I Love You present."

"Yeah." I hugged that cow-ears headband. The only cow-ears

headband in the whole second grade.

Mallory and I lined up next to each other for going in from recess.

"I never got an I Love You present," Mallory whispered.

"I never did before, either," I whispered back.

"I hope I get one someday," Mallory whispered.

Chapter
51

"Want to try it on?" I asked Mallory.

"Yes," Mallory whispered. "But I don't want to ruin it with my Lion Hair full of shampoo."

"It'll be okay," I said.

"You don't think your Gingy and Poopsie would be mad?"

"No," I said, imagining their faces.
Proud faces.

"I think they'd be happy."

"Let's try on each other's," Mallory
suggested.

"Okay," I said, and we did.

"We look great," Mallory said.

"We both look great!" I said.

We jumped around so happy
together.

*Sorry I let my nasty thoughts out,
Mallory,* I thought.

But it was too hard to let that nice sentence out right then.

Maybe sometimes it's okay to keep your nice sentences inside your private head, too.

I don't know.

I was too busy jumping around in a circle with Mallory to decide about that.

Chapter
52

We walked in from recess together.

Before we got in, I asked Mallory for my cow-ears headband back.

I put it on my head.

It wasn't too squishy anymore.

It was perfect.

Chapter 53

When we got back into Class 2B,
Ms. Patel had great news!

It was time to make our Leaf
Collage!

Everybody's leaves looked
different.

But they were all beautiful.

We did some good arranging.

We gave each other space.

We used a lot of glue.

It looked great.

Like us.

Acknowledgments

With thanks and love to:

Amy Berkower, Elizabeth's friend and defender (and mine)

Elizabeth's best friends at Feiwel & Friends:

Anna Roberto, Elizabeth's new superhero

Liz Dresner, designer of the beautiful cover and interior

Starr Baer, star of the schedule/copyediting/proofreading

Molly Brouillette, who takes care of all things publicity and marketing

Kim Waymer, who manages everything to do with producing the actual book

Melissa Croce, who gets Elizabeth to libraries and schools—some of her favorite places

And of course, forever, Liz Szabla and Jean Feiwel

Paige Keiser, gentle artist extraordinaire

Meg, brightener of moods and afternoons, by and in text

Zachary and Liam, who make me smile, snack, and be funnier

Nina, who live-texted as she read this
book, which swelled my heart

Hannah, Emily, Isaac, Adam, Sarah,
Katrina, Bex, Simon, Syd, Simone, Jason,
Stephen, Pen, Xan, and other beloveds
who share their hilarious stories with me
(including my newest nephew, JT: Welcome to
the fam!)

Mom and Dad, who let me cut my hair,
get a headband, prove my point, wear the
costume—and always still saw ME. Still do.

Auntie Lois, who knew the importance of
accessorizing

Grammy, who made clogs and tea parties
for me just when I needed them

N&P G&G G&P N&P, who conjure love
from smiles, sugar, show tickets, and
showing up

Evan and Jill, Susannah and Eric, Lauren
and Peter, Stacy, Lynn, Bea, Tania, Melissa
and Jeff, Stef and Jay, Carin, Mer, Gillian,
Marji, Audrey, Tracy, Mira and Timo, fellow
parents from HCES/TS@C/STUY, and all the
others in life and online who share the stories,
love, frustrations, and laughs of trying to be
the parents our kids need—and reminding one
another when we inevitably fall short that our
kids are awesome anyway.

Thank you for reading this Feiwel and Friends book.

The Friends who made

at Ears on

ELIZABETH

possible are:

Jean Feiwel, Publisher

Liz Szabla, Associate Publisher

Rich Deas, Senior Creative Director

Holly West, Senior Editor

Anna Roberto, Senior Editor

Kat Brzozowski, Senior Editor

Alexei Esikoff, Senior Managing Editor

Kim Waymer, Senior Production Manager

Erin Siu, Associate Editor

Emily Settle, Associate Editor

Rachel Diebel, Assistant Editor

Foyinsi Adegbonmire, Editoral Assistant

Liz Dresner, Associate Art Director

Starr Baer, Associate Copy Chief

Follow us on Facebook or visit us online at mackids.com

Our books are friends for life.